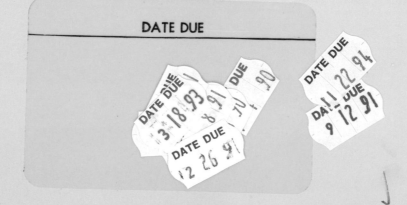

DOVE ISABEAU

WRITTEN BY

JANE YOLEN

ILLUSTRATED BY

DENNIS NOLAN

HARCOURT BRACE JOVANOVICH, PUBLISHERS

SAN DIEGO   NEW YORK   LONDON

Library of Congress Cataloging-in-Publication Data
Yolen, Jane.
Dove Isabeau/by Jane Yolen: illustrated by Dennis Nolan. — 1st ed.
p.   cm.
Summary: Young, beautiful Dove Isabeau is turned into
a fire-breathing dragon by her evil stepmother and is
saved from the spell by her true love, Kemp Owain.
ISBN 0-15-224131-0
[1. Fairy tales.] I. Nolan, Dennis, ill.   II. Title.
PZ8.Y78Do 1989
[Fic] — dc19   88-21333

First edition   A B C D E

The illustrations in this book were done in Windsor-Newton
watercolors on Arches watercolor paper.
The display type was hand-lettered by the artist, based on Goudy Old Style.
The text type was set in Cochin Roman with Cloister Italics
by Thompson Type, San Diego, California.
Printed and bound by Tien Wah Press, Singapore
Production supervision by Warren Wallerstein and Rebecca Miller Garcia
Designed by Joy Chu

TO MARILYN, BONNIE, AND WILLA,
WHO HAVE THE FIRE BENEATH THE SKIN
— J. Y.

TO ANDY, WHO HAS LEARNED
THE GOOD MAGICKS
— D.N.

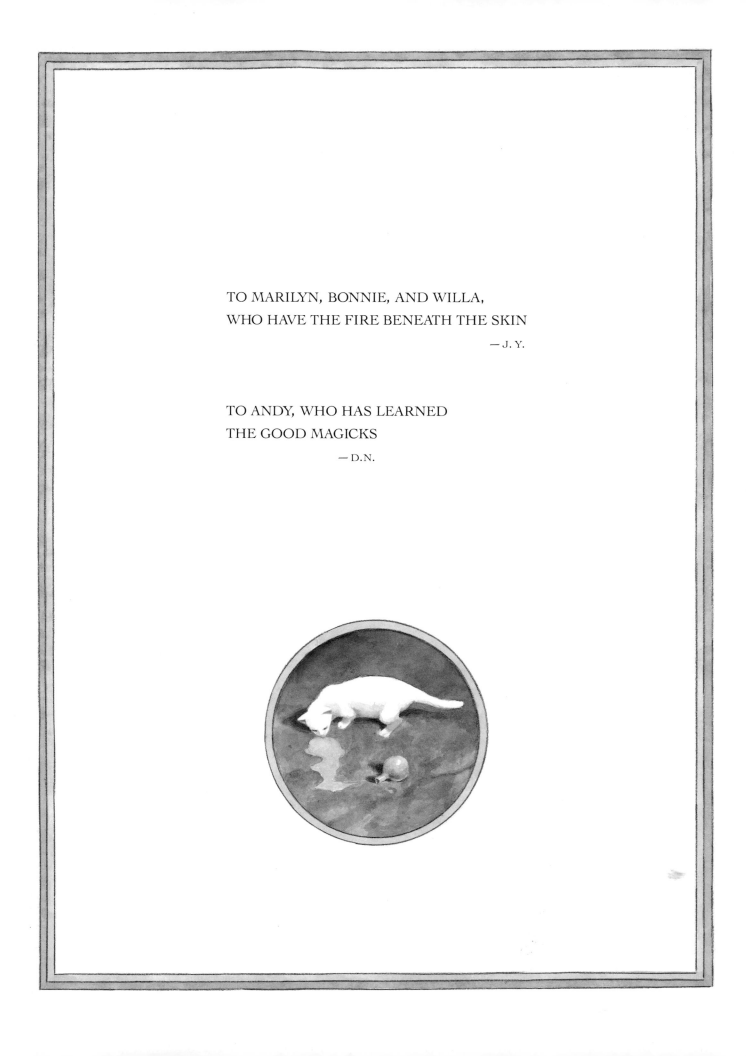

O N THE COLD NORTHERN SHORE OF CRAIG'S COVE, where the trees bear leaves only three months of the year, there stood a great stone castle with three towers. In the central tower lived a girl named Isabeau, and she was fair.

Her hair was the color of the tops of waves when the sun lights them from above, and her eyes were as dark blue as the sea. Her figure was slender, her hands gentle, her fingers slim and fine. She spoke with a voice that was clear and low. And because she always dressed in gray or white, the color of a dove, she was known as Dove Isabeau.

All the young men in the kingdom loved her, gardener and guardsman alike. They loved her for her gentle nature, her lovely face, and her fine form. But no one loved her more than the king's son, Kemp Owain. He had been sent beyond the sea for several years to get learning and to study the great magicks. All his boyhood he had loved Dove Isabeau; he had always looked beyond her face and gentle form, loving her for her spirit and for the fire that lay beneath the skin.

One hard winter, when Isabeau was fourteen, her mother took sick, an illness that turned her own considerable beauty to sores and scales and brought her great suffering. All that was left her was her voice, sweet and pure. Isabeau and her father, Lord Darnton, tended her day and night, and Lady Darnton's little white cat especially never left her side. But Isabeau's mother died at last, when winter had a hold on both the land and their hearts.

Lord Darnton married again in the summer, all too hastily, because he needed to believe in life again. The woman he wed had eyes the green of May but a heart as bleak as February. Unknown to Isabeau and her father, the woman was a witch. Her magic was as deep as the waters of the Craig. She was jealous of youth; she was jealous of beauty; she was jealous of Dove Isabeau.

She disguised her coldness behind soft slow smiles, but the servants were not fooled. They heard her talking aloud in her tower room when she thought none of them were about:

> *Silver glass, my only friend,*
> *Show me how Dove's life shall end.*
> *Great and great my hate does grow*
> *For the lovely Isabeau.*

A hanging ball of glass twisted in the window, turning first black, then white. She waited to see what picture the ball would show her, a picture that would spell out the fate she asked of it. But it showed her only the landscape of her own heart, as hard and unyielding as the tumbled rocks of the cove.

Dove Isabeau missed her own mother dreadfully. She had terrible dreams at night. So she tried to please her father's new wife, giving all to her that she wished she could still give to her mother. She served the woman breakfast each morning in the great curtained bed. She washed her stepmother's undergarments in the cold streams with her own hands.

But nothing Isabeau did pleased the woman, and, at last, the stepmother barred Isabeau and the white cat from her room with one of those soft smiles that disguised her true heart.

Isabeau, with the cat in her arms, descended the tower stairs feeling as if she had, indeed, buried her mother and her own life in the same box.

Silently, the cat licked Isabeau's hand.

But the witch did not mind the hurt she had given. Just as she did every night, she consulted the hanging glass ball, speaking to it in the hushed tones of a conspirator. But because she did not see an answer in the glass, the witch left Isabeau alone.

One night, when the full moon shone through the window of the witch's tower room, a small frightened lizard climbed down the chain and across the face of the glass ball. In the room of shadows, he seemed a part of the picture in the glass. The witch read the message there — for magic has its own strange alphabet — and she laughed aloud.

"Oh, Isabeau, I have you now. No longer dove, no longer loved, you shall be as cold and hard as the rocks of Craig's Cove, even as I am." She took the little lizard by the tail and flung it out the window onto the stones below.

Then, guided by moonlight, she made her way down the cliffs. There she gathered sea polyps from the water and dark moss that clung to the rocks. Inland she picked pennyroyal, henbane, chervil, and rue. It was late into the night when she made her way back to the house, her apron filled with the herbs of devilry.

All the servants and Lord Darnton were fast asleep. But Isabeau, troubled by dreams, was downstairs, awake. She opened the castle door to the witch.

"My dear new mother!" cried Isabeau in alarm. "Your gown is wet and trailing mud. Your eyes are red and worn. Is anything the matter?"

The witch smiled coldly. "Come up to my room, child, and I will show you what I have here in my apron."

They were the first kind words she had spoken, and Isabeau was grateful.

"I will be up at once," she said. "Though first I must bar the door."

"Bar the door," the witch said, still smiling. Turning away she added under her breath, "For all the good it will do."

But Isabeau did not hear that, and she gladly pushed the wooden bolt home. A sliver pricked her finger, and her cry brought the little white cat, who came up and licked the wound clean. It healed as if by magic.

They went upstairs together, the stepmother in the lead, and all the house quiet about them. The white cat followed, careful not to be seen. Its fur was all rumpled and full of dirt, for it had been trailing the stepmother all night long.

In the tower room, Dove Isabeau looked about in surprise. It was no longer the bright, cheery room her mother had loved, with its tapestries of dancing maidens, the spinning wheel and embroidery frames, the baskets filled with skeins of wool. Now it was a place of dark magicks: the great wooden table held beakers, bowls, and books; herbs dried from hooks in the wooden beams; and, though it was midsummer's eve, a fire blazed in the hearth, with a black cauldron at the boil.

"Stand there, child," the witch said, pointing to a rug on the floor emblazoned with a great red star. "Stand there that I may better see your lovely face."

Unsuspecting, Isabeau did as her stepmother asked, stepping into the very center of the star. She turned her face from the window, where the last lines of night were just stretching into dawn.

The witch waved her hands three times in Isabeau's direction before the girl could protest. And then it was too late. Isabeau could no longer move at all.

Flinging the herbs into Isabeau's face, the witch cried out:

Herbs of evil, herbs of woe,
Change the shape of Isabeau.

A river of fire suddenly ran through Isabeau's veins. Her breath grew strong; her nails grew long. Her hair lengthened into a tangled mane. A reddish scale grew over her face and arms and legs. From between her shoulders, bursting the careful stitches of her gown, great pinioned wings began to sprout. And stretching behind her was a sinuous, twisting tail.

"Go, Wyrm!" the witch cried triumphantly. "Wind yourself around the rocks upon which this castle stands. What man will look at you now, my dove? What heart will love you? When you were innocent and fair to behold, you held every man's affection. But in this twisted, scaly form you will command no kisses—only curses and the point of a sword. Even your father will despise you. When all the young men have died beneath your claws, and even the king's son, Kemp Owain, is killed, then I shall claim first this castle and then this kingdom for my own."

The witch began to laugh and spin around the room. She danced with shadows and bowed to the waning moon. As she did so, the great red dragon that had been Dove Isabeau began to move. She climbed clumsily out the window and coasted down on untried wings to settle on the cold stones.

And the little white cat crept away down the stairs, careful not to be seen.

Morning came, a pale sun rising, shrouded by clouds. But even more shrouded were the stones of the castle around which the great red dragon wrapped itself.

Inside, Lord Darnton and all the servants felt their blood thin out; their bones grow brittle; their heartbeats slow. They grew weaker with each passing hour as if the dragon were draining them of all life.

That day, when the young men of the kingdom came, one by one, to court Isabeau, the sight of the dragon—with its fierce red jaws, its mighty pinions, and its cruel, slashing claws—sent each of them galloping home afraid.

But later, shamed, one by one they returned with weapons to slay the wyrm and rescue Isabeau and her father from the dragon's grasp.

On the high road to the great stone castle, each suitor was met by the little white cat, who mewed piteously and tried to bar the way. One by one the young men drove it off with blows and curses, eager to kill the giant wyrm.

But however they tried to slay it, by spear or by stake, by sword or by bow, the young men died as young men will: foolishly, carelessly, bravely, and well. No one was left to watch the red beast weep as it gnawed upon their bones.

Under the dragon's shadow, Lord Darnton's castle and the entire kingdom seemed doomed.

At last Kemp Owain was summoned by his frightened father. He returned from across the sea.

"Oh, my son," the king said, "a great, hideous dragon circles the place where Lord Darnton and Isabeau dwell. There is a terrible dark sorcery there. None of the young men of the kingdom has succeeded in slaying the wyrm. Nine and ninety have gone out. Not one has returned."

Kemp Owain nodded. "Dark sorcery indeed," he said. He saddled his good gray horse and put a sword and dagger at his waist. "Father, if I, who know the good magicks, do not return, let no one else come. For it will mean that I, and Isabeau, and all her house are dead."

Then he kissed his mother and father good-bye, mounted his horse, and rode off toward the north shore of the Craig.

As he turned onto the high road, the little white cat crossed before him. The horse shied, and it was all Kemp Owain could do to keep his seat. But instead of striking at the cat or cursing it, he calmed the horse and dismounted, for he recognized the cat as Lady Darnton's.

"Little catkin," he said, picking it up and stroking its fur, "you must run away and quickly. If that dragon can devour grown men, surely you would be but a single *snick-snack* in its giant maw."

Much to his surprise, the cat began to speak in Lady Darnton's sweet, pure voice.

If the sword bites tail or fin,
Isabeau you will not win.

If the sword bites wing or tail,
Isabeau you'll surely fail.
But give the red wyrm kisses three,
And Isabeau you shall set free.

Now, as Kemp Owain knew sorcery, he was sure that that verse was not all there was to the spell.

"What more, catkin?" he asked.

Giving a soft miaou, the cat leaped from his hands. Looking back over its shoulder, it spoke again.

Give the red wyrm kisses three,
Turned to stone you'll surely be.

Then it ran off down the road toward the castle.

Kemp Owain rode after the cat. As he got closer, he could see the dragon's bright red scales flashing in the sun. Without thinking, he rode straight for the front gate. But catching the dragon's smell, his horse reared suddenly, and Kemp Owain was thrown to the ground. He got to his feet, threw off his cape, and drew his sword. The dragon unwrapped itself from the rocky face of the middle tower and launched its giant body into the air.

As the wyrm hovered above him, Kemp Owain saw that whenever he raised his sword, the dragon advanced. But when he lowered it, the dragon retreated.

Then the white cat's words came back to him:

> *If the sword bites tail or fin,*
> *Isabeau you will not win.*
> *If the sword bites wing or tail,*
> *Isabeau you'll surely fail.*

Once more he raised his sword. Roaring fire and smoke, the dragon plunged down toward him.

Kemp Owain drew a great breath. He knew what he had to do. Using more courage than he thought he had, he threw the sword away. The dragon banked suddenly and flew off.

Staring through the smoke, Kemp Owain thought he saw only dragon, all talons and tail and teeth. Then, remembering his lessons in sorcery, he squinted his eyes and looked *beneath* the wyrm form. There he saw the faint outline of a slim, fair girl. She was weeping tears of blood.

"Dove Isabeau," he whispered. And slowly, so as not to alarm the dragon, he took the knife from his waist and threw it away as well.

"Come, wyrm or dove," he called, his voice shaking. "I would give you a token of my love." Then he opened his arms to his death.

The dragon dove straight for him, pulling up only at the last to backwing frantically and settle down by his side, When it landed, it shook the earth. Its head was as high as the rooftree of a house, its middle he could not have spanned. Its jaws were large enough to roast an entire ox. In its burnished scales, Kemp Owain could read his own face a hundred times.

He closed his eyes and was bending over to kiss the great beast on the mouth when he suddenly remembered the other words the little cat had said:

Give the red wyrm kisses three,
Turned to stone you'll surely be.

But it was already too late to change his mind. His lips touched the dragon's lips. And though he had expected the thin, cold mouth of a serpent, the touch was as warm and soft as a girl's. Not knowing what to expect, he opened his eyes. The dragon was still there before him, but a coldness was spreading up from his feet. When he looked down, he saw that he had turned to stone from his toes to his waist.

What had he done? The dragon was unchanged, but *he* was surely lost. Still, what did his own life matter? It was Isabeau he must free and the kingdom he must save. He stared through the haze of dragon smoke and scale to the weeping girl beneath and kissed the dragon a second time.

The dragon's mouth was warmer still, but Kemp Owain felt the coldness spreading throughout his body, turning it to stone from waist to neck. Yet he could feel the beating of his own steady heart beneath the stone.

The dragon turned its sad, dark, weeping eyes on him.

"Do not mourn for me, wyrm," Kemp Owain cried. "I only do what must be done."

Then, for the third time, he closed his eyes and readied himself for the dragon's kiss.

Since he could no longer move, the dragon came to him, its massive

head gentle against his own. And this kiss was the sweetest kiss of all, for it was the last thing Kemp Owain knew.

No sooner did their lips meet for the third time than the dragon's scales began to drop away. The dragon form peeled open, and from its center stepped Isabeau. She wrapped herself in Kemp Owain's cape.

Her hair was as light as the tops of waves, but her eyes were as dark as the sea. She touched Kemp Owain gently on his stone cheek and felt a tear beneath her fingers.

"I shall avenge you, Kemp Owain," she whispered to his stone ears. Picking up his dagger and sword, she marched into the house.

Isabeau mounted the steps two at a time till she came to the tower room. The witch was standing by the window, staring into her crystal globe. When Isabeau came through the door, a thousand tiny cracks jetted around the glass ball.

Looking up, the witch laughed, "So, Isabeau, you are to be my death. The glass did not tell me, but I can read it in your eyes. You could not have done it before. You had not the right fire for it, nor the blood. But what runs in your veins now is the legacy of all those rash young men you devoured. Yet know this—whatever you do, Kemp Owain is lost. Only the blood of the innocent young girl you once were can bring him back." She laughed and laughed until the walls of the tower room rang with the sound.

Isabeau gave an awful cry, part dragon's curse, part maiden's prayer. She flung the dagger as hard as she could. It hit the witch in the shoulder with such force she staggered back, tumbled through the open window, and fell to the rocks below.

Though Isabeau could not bear to look down, she hurled the sword after.

For a long moment she waited for the sound of sword on stone. When it did not come, she smiled the dragon's smile and went back down the stairs. Opening the front doors, she walked to the statue of Kemp Owain and stared at it for a long, long time.

  She was still standing there when Lord Darnton found her. With
him were all the members of his household. Isabeau was weeping as if
her tears might wash away the stone.

  Just then the little white cat rubbed against her ankles. She picked it
up and stroked its silken head. Remembering how it had once licked
the blood from her hand when the wooden sliver had pricked her,
Isabeau cried: "Alas, catkin, that was the last bit of innocent blood I
will ever shed! If only I could have it back. I would give it all, every
drop, to have Kemp Owain alive and whole."

  "The wish is the deed," purred the cat in a familiar voice, both sweet
and pure. "And so breaks the spell."

The white cat leaped from Isabeau's hands and ran to the statue, where it began licking the feet. The cat licked and licked until it had worn away the outer stone, revealing to them what lay beneath. There stood Kemp Owain, alive and only slightly dazed, remembering nothing after the dragon's final kiss.

What feasting and celebration occurred then, for seven days and seven nights, until they were all thoroughly tired of it. And when Kemp Owain and Dove Isabeau were married, the cat was the happiest celebrant of them all, with its own silver bowl of cream and a dozen small sprats caught fresh from the cove. And never a word more did it speak but *miaou*.

Much to the surprise of all the guests, Isabeau wore neither white nor gray for the wedding. Instead she dressed in a gown of red. And after, though others still called her Dove Isabeau, remembering her innocent past, Kemp Owain did not. Delighting in her spirit and fire, which he had always known was hidden beneath her gentle form, he called her his fierce guardian, his mighty warrior, and his glorious dragon queen for all the long, happy years they ruled the kingdom together.